BIG**FAT**

Special Delivery

Hedonist

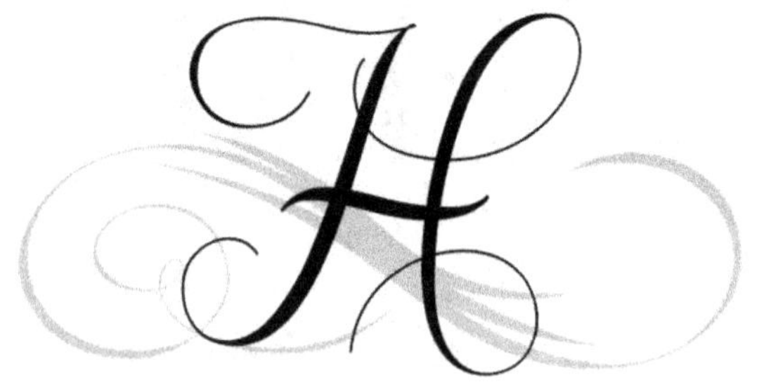

Hedonist

CONTENTS

BIG FAT SPECIAL DELIVERY

I make my way to the door and knock. No answer. I transfer the heavy tray of frappuccinos from one hand to the other and wipe the sweat off my brow with the back of my hand. This better not be a fucking prank. I swear,if this is some kind of joke, I'm dumping all this stuff on the floor right here. No way am I carrying everything back to the cafe. It's anyway paid for already.

I knock again, and finally, I hear a bit of a rustle on the other side of the door.

"It's open."

Sure enough, when I turn the knob, it unlocks readily, allowing me to push the door open with my elbow.

"Hi, I've got your order here," I say, while peeping inside. It's dark, so I can't see much of anything. But the smell… Jesus. It's ripe in there. Like stale locker room mixed in with something weirdly sweet which I can't identify.

"Uhh thanks," a male voice speaks. "On the table, please."

I crinkle my nose and push the door open some more with my hip. Ah, there's the table, right by the door. Where's the customer, though? The guy who was just speaking to me?

I put the tray down, and then the bag of sandwiches that's been hanging off my arm, cutting deeply into my skin. I rub the indent it made, but it still stings.

"Can you unpack it for me?" that same voice asks. His tone is apologetic, almost like he's regretting his request as soon as he completes it.

"Sure," I mumble, while taking the drinks off the tray and arranging them neatly side-by-side. Six super-sized Frapps. And then the sandwiches. I get them out of the bag and pile them into a pyramid shape in the center of the table.

"Having a party?" I ask. Though I can't imagine many people would like to come here, considering what the place smells like.

The man doesn't respond. All I can hear is heavy breathing somewhere on the other side of the room. The hairs on the back of my neck stand up. Maybe this was a mistake. Have I inadvertently walked into some Jeffrey Dahmer wannabe's kill lair? Is he going to sneak up on me from behind and jump me before I get the chance to escape?

I turn around, and check for where he must be, ready to bolt if necessary. My eyes have become used to the dim lighting, so now I can see a bit better than when I first entered.

I'm captivated by two eyes, staring at me from across the room. Two pleading eyes, roughly at my chest level. God, he looks so sad.

Why isn't he coming over here to get his food? I pause for a moment, and look around the room some more. It's dingy; cluttered; dirty… Almost like nobody really lives here.

He still hasn't moved from his position in what looks

like a big old fashioned armchair.

"Umm, anything else?" I wonder aloud.

He shakes his head. I think I see tears glistening in his eyes. Shit, he seems to captivate me, with nothing more than just a gaze.

"Well, you paid online, so I guess that's me done then," I mumble.

"Actually…" He tries to clear his throat, which makes him cough, which in turn makes his breathing even more laboured. It scares me. Whoever he is; I don't think he's doing very well.

"Yes?"

"Could you—" his breaths have turned into wheezes now. Is this guy okay? "—bring that table over here?"

"Sure thing," I whisper, while tugging at the table. Huh; it moves rather easily. I hadn't even noticed it was on wheels before.

That weird sweetish smell gets stronger as I approach him, but there's also something else. Ammonia. And then the reason for his odd request becomes apparent. He *is* sitting in an armchair. But he's pretty much so big, he fills it out so completely, there's hardly a gap around him. Almost like he's wearing it on his backside, rather than simply sitting in it.

"Umm…" I stare down at his thick legs, which are almost spilling out of the front end of the chair in an awkward position. His stomach, which strains against a sweat-stained t-shirt with every laboured breath, is almost broader than the opening of the chair itself. "Are you okay?"

He nods, while reaching for the first drink with a tremble in his hand. Suddenly his focus has shifted from me, to the food. He barely hesitates, just starts sucking at the straw as hard as he can. His eyes close when the liquid makes it into his mouth, swallowing eagerly, until the first brain freeze hits him.

Ice is the secret to a thick frappuccino. And for deliveries, extra ice.

He groans and stops for a brief moment, but then he carries on as if his life depends on it. In between coughs and gasps for air, he downs the whole thing in under a minute. My heart is racing and my palms are sweating profusely. I'm still on high alert, and completely baffled by what I've found here in this unassuming flat.

"You're thirsty, huh?" I mumble.

What the hell am I looking at, over here? This man; early thirties maybe, so big it looks like he would not be able to get up out of that chair... His clothes; the smell; his ravenous appetite. I can feel my heart hammering all the way up in my throat.

It's 10:35 in the morning. My first order of the day, which came in as soon as we opened. I thought it would be rather routine; a mid-morning work meeting, maybe. But this... This is not what I signed up for. This here is something you might see in a horror movie, except he doesn't look like the villain, but like a victim instead.

On the floor around him, I see a slew of empty pizza boxes, and even more Chinese takeout containers. There is also a sizable collection of 2 Litre Coke bottles. Some are empty. Some partially filled with... something that isn't coke judging by the colour of it. All look like they've been in here a while, covered in a thin yet even layer of dust.

How long has he been sitting here, without fresh food or water? I don't see a phone nearby. How in the name of hell did he place these orders without one?

"Hey, what's your name?" I ask.

He's shivering when he puts the now empty glass down on his thigh and stares at me again. There's something in his eyes that keeps me standing right there, frozen in place. I don't feel threatened anymore, because I realize I have all the power in this situation whereas he has none.

"Zach."

"I'm Lindsay."

The helpless look in his eyes sends shivers down my spine now. This is wrong. This whole situation is so very wrong. How long has this been going on? And how did he get this way?

"Zach, umm… Are you sure you're okay?"

"Fine, yeah." He coughs again. His whole body shakes and jiggles as he does. His legs don't budge an inch though. Yeah. He's fucking stuck. Why didn't he say something? By now I could have called for help already.

He gestures at me to bring the sandwiches closer. I grab one in each hand, almost on autopilot. He takes the first one and unwraps it, then he takes a big bite. He barely chews before swallowing. It's like watching one of those car crushing machines at the scrap yard. Bite, chew twice, swallow, repeat. After finishing the first of what are admittedly quite big sandwiches, he tries to reach for another, but he can't, because I'm standing just a little too far away from him.

I should probably go. Mind my own business. But I'm frozen in place, just watching him.

As he tries to lean forward to grab the second sandwich from my hands, he coughs even more. At this rate, he might just choke on a piece of bread.

If I don't do anything and just get the hell out of here, he's definitely going to choke, and his death will be on my conscience.

"Zach, do me a favour," I say.

His eyes water as he strains for air. But luckily, one big cough later, he's able to breathe again.

"You should go," he says. "Just leave the table next to me, okay?"

"Yeah…" I look around the depressing room again. Then I grab my phone from my pocket, and stare at it, unsure of what to do next.

"What are you doing?" he asks.

"I think you need some help. I should call for help," I conclude.

"Stop! Don't do that!" He reaches over and tries to grab my phone. He can't reach, of course. Still, I take a step back, just to be sure. If by some kind of miracle he manages to get up out of that chair, I'll leave him to it.

But otherwise… There's no way in hell I'm walking away now.

"Come on now," I say. "You're obviously stuck. And

you're eating that sandwich like you haven't eaten in days."

He makes a face and looks away. "I don't see how that's any of your business."

"Well, it wasn't, until you asked me in and I saw—" I can't help but crinkle my nose again. Saw and smelled. "—the situation. It became my business as soon as I walked through the door."

"Please don't call anyone."

"Why?" I ask.

"Because."

"That's not an answer."

"He told me to wait for him here—"

"Someone else lives here with you? Someone who takes care of you?"

He nods and looks up at me again with tear-filled eyes. Is he shitting me right now? Someone else lives in this hellhole? Someone who couldn't be bothered to pick up all this crap off the floor and feed him on a regular basis? Or at the very least help him out of this predicament, so he could fetch things for himself?

"This is just temporary. It'll soon be over." He sniffles once, then picks up the next frappuccino off of the table. I'm not sure I like the sound of that last statement. And I'm not sure I believe him that there's someone else coming. Certainly not someone capable of helping him or caring for him. Otherwise why did they let it get to this point?

"Zach, slow down. What will soon be over?" I ask.

He shivers and blinks a few times as he puts the

drink down. It's way too cold to be drinking that fast. He must have one killer headache already. "All of it. This is just a test."

"Well, how long has he been gone?"

He thinks for a moment before answering, then he scans the boxes on the floor. "He got me pizza."

I pick up the nearest box. As luck would have it, the receipt is still stuck to the outside of the lid. It's dated four days ago. My heart breaks. He's been sitting here in the dark by himself for four fucking days?

"You've–" I shudder to think of it even. "Zach, you're telling me, the last time you saw anyone was when this pizza came?"

"Yeah. But today he got me all of this." He points at the stuff I brought. What the actual fuck? But there's nobody else here, though. Does this mean…

"Did he literally bring you this pizza, or did the pizza get delivered as well?"

I really don't like the sound of his breaths. This is a man in need of actual medical care; I'm not equipped for this.

"He…" He closes his mouth without finishing the sentence. He's lying. He knows I know he's lying. The pizza was delivered. And it follows that the Chinese food was also delivered, who knows how many days prior.

And it's obvious that he can't get up, that's why the empty containers are just lying around like this. Which explains the smell. How the fuck has he been going to the bathroom if he can't get up? I shudder to think of it.

"I'm sorry." He shakes his head. "It must stink in here."

"Zach, how long have you been sitting in this chair right here?" I whisper.

His tears are flowing steadily now. He must feel so ashamed. So far, he'd been pretending with me, but I'm shattering his denial with my questions. He knows now that I know what's happening.

"I…"

"Zach, it's okay. It's going to be okay." I take a couple of steps forward and put my hand on his shoulder.

He might be in a disgusting state, but he's still human after all. And I can't bear to just watch.

"Don't touch me," he cries.

I flinch away.

"Zach, sweetheart, you need help," I tell him.

He carries on shaking his head. "No. He'll come for me. He promised."

"Who is he?"

"Jared."

"Okay… And is he family, or…?"

He sniffles loudly, which makes him cough, which in turn makes him throw up some of the frappuccino he's been downing. He tries to force it back, but some of it dribbles down his chin. In hindsight, that's an obvious side-effect of what's happening. He can't be eating and drinking like this in his state. Not this quickly, and certainly not all at once.

"I'm so sorry," he says, while wiping his face with

the back of his hand, then staring down at it in disgust.

"Zach, you haven't had any food for days. You need to take it easy," I tell him, while sliding the table back from his chair.

"No, don't!" He tries reaching for it, but he can't anymore. "No!"

"It's super dangerous to overeat after you've been starving, Zach. I need you to believe me."

The look in his eyes is sheer despair. It nearly breaks me. Am I literally taking food away from a starving man right now? It's for his own good, though.

"Please tell me who Jared is. If you won't let me call anyone else, at least tell me how to contact him?"

"No way! He'll be mad if he finds out I've been talking to you."

I frown. This just keeps on getting scarier and scarier. I should stop arguing with this guy and just call the police. Or the fire department. Or, I don't even know who. In any case, I've got to *do* something.

"He doesn't like you talking to delivery people? When you literally need them to come in and hand you the food?" No matter what he says now; how he tries to brush it away, I'm convinced this Jared person is trying to hurt him. That's why he said it'll be over soon.

"Look, I'm going to call my boss and tell him I'm not coming back in today. We're going to figure this out together."

"Why? You made the delivery now. Just go already."

"Fuck that. Zach, listen to me. I'm not leaving you alone. Not like this."

He stares up at me, his mouth slightly agape, then he starts to protest again. "No, no, no, this is wrong. He won't like this at all. No, you have to go now!"

His irrational ramblings are starting to get on my nerves now. I square off against him with both arms propped up against my hips. "Great. Make me. Get up and push me out the door and I'll go."

"Please." His voice is so low, it threatens to break me again. I don't let it show, though.

"Get up and make me!" He flinches when I raise my voice.

Then, he takes a deep-ish rattly breath and starts to push down on the armrests. The chair groans as he tries to shift his weight, but it continues to hold him captive. He goes red in the face as he carries on struggling.

"I didn't think so. I didn't think you could!" I taunt him. Who knows, maybe if I rile him up enough, the adrenaline might just do the trick and this will all sort itself out somehow.

"Fuck!" He cries out as he slumps back against the chair with his eyes flagging and sweat dripping down his sideburns and messy beard. All he's managed to do is get himself wedged in tighter.

"Now, if I've proven my point, we're going to do things my way," I tell him.

His eyes flick open as he looks up at me again.

"He'll kill me."

"He's already killing you. If I hadn't stopped you from eating the rest of the food, that would have surely done it," I argue.

He longingly stares at the table, still overloaded with sandwiches. And four more frappuccinos. Just the caffeine alone… I dread to think of what could have happened here. If I'd just left the food here in front of him and gone… He would have been a headline in the papers. Morbidly obese man found dead in his apartment after apparently getting stuck in chair.

And likely nobody would have thought twice about it. People would make mean remarks about self-control and gluttony, feeling all superior about not ever getting into that kind of a situation themselves, and gone about their day as normal.

But I would have known that he was alive when I brought his delivery. I would have known that I was the last person who saw him before he passed away. All alone in this filthy room, choking on a piece of bread.

And I don't know how I could live with something like that.

No. I have to help him. And I'd like to help him without upsetting him further, or he might just end up having a heart attack or something. So, until I gain some of his trust, I'm going to help him myself.

With this newfound resolve spurring me on, I roll the table away a little further, and start exploring his place.

"Where are you going?" he calls after me.

"I'm going to help you, whether you like it or not." I tap out a quick message to cancel the rest of my shift while wandering off.

"Don't go in there!" he says, when I approach the

small hallway leading away from this room.

I don't listen. At least it smells a tiny bit better in here, even if the entire apartment is covered in dust and grime.

There's a bedroom, which nobody has seemingly set foot in for ages, a kitchen that nobody has cooked in for even longer, and a bathroom that looks somewhat passable, just dusty. Armed with a bucket of warm water, some soap, and a somewhat clean washcloth, I make my way back into the living room. Then I make another trip to the kitchen for a glass of water, into which I mix some sugar and a pinch of salt. I've heard that electrolytes are super important when you've been stranded without food and water for a while. This surely counts as a similar situation.

He doesn't say anything when I reappear, there's just the slightly irregular rhythm of his breaths filling the room. I glance over at him and see that his eyes are half-shut. Maybe all the exertion of trying to get out of the chair has been a bit much for him. Still, as long as he's breathing, that's fine. And if he's passed out, at least he won't carry on complaining about what I'm up to.

First, I make room around the chair, clearing away the trash off the floor and dumping it in a corner.

"Zach, I'm going to have to touch you now," I tell him.

His eyes open wide when I take the washcloth, dipped in warm water and soap, and carefully dab his face with it to clean up the rest of the vomit.

"What the–" he complains, then coughs again. Why

is he coughing so damn much? Is he sick? Maybe it's the fumes in here. Or this awkward posture he's been stuck in for so long.

"It's okay, Zach."

"Please don't touch me," he cries out and flinches when I dab the towel against his neck, throat, and along the front of his t-shirt where a fresh stain of vomit has formed. "He won't like it!"

"Give me your hands," I demand.

He does it, despite his repeated protests. They're still trembling and weak despite their large size.

I gently wash him with the wet towel. First one arm and hand, then the other. He's panting furiously throughout the whole thing and flinching with every touch. As if it hurts him. How can it, when I'm being ever so gentle?

"We're going to have to get you out of this chair somehow. How long ago did this happen?"

He stares at me, blankly. I don't think he knows for sure how much time has passed.

"I can get up. Anytime I want."

"Okay, Zach." I shake my head while trying to wrack my brain for possible solutions.

Someone as big as him would usually sit with his legs splayed to allow for his gut to sit in between. I've seen guys his size come into the cafe before and that's usually what it looks like. That way he'd be able to lean forward to transfer his weight onto his feet. But he's just wedged in there tight with his legs together.

As for his feet… They're not even flat on the ground

right now. Would they even be able to carry his weight?

Maybe… If I manage to remove one of the armrests somehow…

While thinking through various options, I hand him the glass of water, which he gulps down eagerly. I don't even try to tell him to take it easy. It's probably a safer bet than the fraps he's already consumed and might prevent anything really bad from happening.

Instead, I focus my attention back on the chair. I feel around the fabric and padding to see if it has any give. There isn't much. Armed with a half-baked plan and a stubborn desire to actually help him in a real way, I leave the living room again and start looking around his house for some tools. There isn't much. A couple of kitchen knives and one of those folding multi-tools are all I can find.

"Shit, what are you doing?" he calls out when he spots the big knives in my hand.

"I'm going to get you out."

"No, you can't. He wants me to stay here and wait for him."

"I know you don't want to accept this, but I'm not convinced he's coming at all. Whether you wait here or not."

He presses his lips together tight, but a loud sob still escapes them. Maybe that was harsh of me, but he needed to hear the truth.

"Zach, you're okay. I'm not leaving you. Not like he did." I rest my hand on his shoulder, which only makes him erupt more. He shudders under my touch; his whole body jiggling like jelly. He really is quite fat. I wonder if he did that all by himself, or I've walked in on something even more depraved than what it seems like right now. First the bastard fattened him up, got him stuck in this chair, and then left him to die alone once he realised how much trouble he'd be to take care of in any meaningful way... Is this a sick sex thing, like Dahmer? I shudder to think about it. Maybe I should quit watching all these fucked up things on Netflix, because they're messing with my imagination.

Tears sting in my own eyes too now. I lean over and put my arm around his shoulder in an attempt to comfort him. Or maybe myself too, a little. He's not just crying now; he's howling. I can't imagine the pain he's been going through. And the realisation of what's really been going on must be almost as bad as the physical pain.

"I'm sorry Zach. I've got you. You're okay," I tell him.

"You shouldn't– You should get away. I'm disgusting; I'm sorry."

"Shh... I'm not leaving you." I squeeze my arm around him slightly. Just enough to make my point. He continues bawling into my shoulder until the tears wet up a good portion of my shirt. Although he is pretty disgusting in his current state, I kind of like how his big body feels against me. The observation shocks me to my core and makes me withdraw. What the fuck am I even thinking about here? All these speculations about serial killer depravity are dragging me into the abyss too.

Except, I don't want to hurt him. Not even a little. Through all the filth and misery, and yes the humongous size of him, I see a scared little boy, crying out for help. I wish I could just take him into my arms and make all of this better. But I can't. Nothing is going to get better as long as he's stuck like this.

"Let's try and get you out of this chair, okay?"

"No! Don't!"

He's hugging me back with one arm now; one very fleshy, very clammy hand rests on my upper back, right between my shoulder blades.

"Zach, sweetheart. We've got to get you out."

"I'm so hungry! So tired…"

"I know you are. And we'll do something about that, but only once we get you out of this chair."

"You're just going to leave; just like everyone else."

"No. I'm not leaving you." My heart aches for him. I'm starting to realise that this isn't just a thing I can do and then forget about. Leaving him for someone else to deal with isn't an option anymore. Even if I do get him out, that's hardly the end of the problem...

I lean back and look down at his wet face. His eyes look sunken; with big dark circles. His hair is overlong and matted, and his patchy beard is coming through pretty long as well. I don't know how fast facial hair grows, but he hasn't had a shower or a shave in a while. Now that I've cleaned him up a little, he looks even paler than he did before. Except for his lips, which are dark purplish and so chapped, they're actually bleeding a little in places.

But it's not all ugliness that I see. I see beautiful blue eyes to complement the dark blonde of his hair. I see regular features; a strong straight nose and shapely eyebrows and those chapped lips of his, they're really rather full and inviting now that I'm looking at them more closely.

It breaks my heart to think of what all got him to this point. How alone and desperate he must have felt waiting for that asshole to send him food. And to what end? *The end?*

"I promise I won't leave you," I tell him.

The way he's staring at me with those pleading eyes of his does something to me. "Yeah, you will."

"No. Never," I say. And I mean it.

He obviously has no one who cares. No one who loves him. The asshole he keeps referring to may have started simply taking advantage of him, much like a bully would. He might have seen him as someone he can mess around a bit, but things are well beyond even that now. This is torture. Mental, physical, emotional torture. This is psycho level stuff right here. A part of me is surprised he's not here watching him slowly fade away.

Or, if he'd eaten all that food, things might have happened pretty quickly instead. I've read about refeeding syndrome. Things could have gone downhill pretty quickly. In fact, I'm not even entirely sure that he will be able to digest what he did eat just now until I took the rest of it away from him.

"I'm *not* leaving you," I repeat. "I promise."

His grip on my shoulder loosens, allowing me to retreat a little. He's looking faint; his eyes are flagging again and those deeper rattly breaths have started up again. I'm sure he's been so hungry for all these days, he wouldn't have gotten any sleep either.

Just when it looks like he's fully passed out, he jerks awake. "No, no, no, I mustn't sleep!"

What the actual fuck?

"Why not?" I ask him. "What'll happen if you sleep?"

"It's… I'm not supposed to be lazy," he whispers. Shit, he sounds so weak right now. "He doesn't like it when I'm lazy."

"Lazy? You're half dead! And how would he even find out? Is he watching us?"

That last question wasn't even aimed at him anymore. I scan the room again; this time the top of the walls. No cameras. Nothing.

But then, there is a laptop sitting on a small table on the other wall. Its screen is dark, and everything looks dead, except for the small LED next to the charging port. But I know better than to assume anything. That laptop has a webcam pointed right at us. How did I not notice that before?

I let go of Zach's shoulder and get over there. Just in case, I close the screen and unplug the charger. Best of luck watching now, you deranged prick!

"No, you shouldn't have done that!" Zach cries out, but I ignore his protests. That's it. I'm getting him the fuck out of that chair right fucking now.

I grab the biggest one of the knives, and start

attacking the upholstery on the arm rest. It's difficult cutting through the thick fabric, but I manage to make a big gash in it after a few tries. Then, I start pulling it off with my hands. Once you get a good handle on it, the fabric tears with ease.

Within minutes, I've bared the side of the chair down to the foam. That comes off much easier with the knife. A wave of stench hits me from underneath. I guess that answers the question of how he's been going to the bathroom since he's been stuck in there. Through the wooden frame and metal spring construction inside the chair, I can see a dried up pool of brownish mess on the vinyl floor below. I try not to gag and focus my attention on the wooden frame of the armrest instead. I need to get this off somehow.

The multi-tool I found in the kitchen has a little saw attachment. It's woefully inadequate for the job, but it's all I've got. So I start grinding away at the vertical supports from the outside in. Of course, on the inside, his huge body is pushing into the wood quite hard, making it even more difficult to keep sawing. Whatever small gap the mini saw blade manages to make, I get stuck in it as the wood continues flexing out against it. But I keep on trying and end up with the beginnings of a wedge cut out. If I get that done, just the strain every one of his breaths puts on the arm rest should crack whatever wood remains. And once that happens…

He's so tense. He looks terrified. His eyes are shut, and his fingers are dug into the padding on the top of the armrest so hard, his knuckles are white.

And on top of that, my hand starts to ache, holding that stupid little multi-tool. And my arm is getting tired. But I can't give up now. I've got to keep going. For Zach. To prove to him that I'm a woman of my word. To prove that some people are worth relying on, unlike that sadistic bastard, Jared. If that's even his real name.

I place my left hand on top of his and rub it gently.

"You'll be okay."

"None of this is okay," he counters in a choked voice.

Well, I guess that's something we can both agree on. None of this *is* okay. But it will be.

The chair groans and creaks, prompting me to speed up my sawing. Sweat drips down my forehead and into my eyes, but I don't let it stop me no matter how much it stings.

"Push that armrest off, Zach," I tell him.

He strains a little. The angle is unfortunate, but bless him, he tries.

And I try as well, gripping at one of the horizontal supports on the top of the armrest. The wood starts to crack.

"On three," I say. "One, two, three!"

He lets out a groan and pushes. I pull at it from my end. Finally, the wooden support I'd been sawing at starts to splinter, and the armrest moves a good two inches outwards.

Zach is panting, and grabbing at his side which had been quite stuck until a moment ago. I can only imagine how much it must hurt; first to be trapped, and then to be released only slightly.

This small triumph spurs me on to continue my assault on the chair, this time starting a wedge-shaped cut-out on the piece of wood that connects the armrest to the back. I switch hands, and although I'm tired, I'm kind of getting the hang of it. Perhaps it's also easier to get through this bit because it's not flexing quite as hard as the other support.

It takes me another ten minutes of grinding at the wood with the stupid little saw until I've made a wedge that's slightly bigger than the last one. Then, I sit down on the ground, grab at the top of the armrest, and upon placing my feet against the bottom of the chair for leverage, I pull as hard as I can.

Sure enough, the wood gives up and the armrest peels away from Zach's body.

"Holy shit." He carefully tries to move his leg to the side, stretching his knee and ankle, whimpering as he does so. But still, with iron determination, he fights through the stiffness and pain, until for the first time in I don't know how long, his foot ends up sitting somewhat flat on the floor.

"Well done! We should do the other armrest now. Give you more room to move," I say.

He looks down at me, while continuing to stretch his leg, and through the tears, I think I see a glimmer of relief; of hope.

And that's everything. I feel my bottom lip tremble. It's such an emotional moment. But I don't waste time getting back to work. I grab my makeshift tools and crawl around the back of the chair to the other side, where I start stabbing at the fabric of the remaining armrest. It soon gives way, allowing me to tear it off by hand.

Sweat continues to trickle down into my face, and both of my hands are getting more and more tired and sore. But I'm not going to give up now. I start sawing at the vertical wooden support first. Just like the other side. My shoulders are feeling heavy, and my fingers are struggling to keep gripping onto the handle of the multi-tool. But I keep going for what feels like forever. Still, this is nothing compared to how long he's been sitting here without any help.

At last, I'm mostly through the vertical wooden piece. I didn't even bother cutting wedges anymore. Neither do I have the energy nor the patience for extra sawing. I move onto the horizontal piece. Slowly but surely chipping away at it. My blade is getting blunt. That must be the reason it's getting so difficult. Eventually I can feel it wobbling a little. With whatever little energy I have left, I pull at it, again using my feet for leverage. It cracks and folds over towards me.

Zach lets out a soft gasp. Relieved, I get onto my feet and observe him stretching his other leg. He's still wedged into what remains of the armrests, but looks so much freer already.

"Making progress," I say.

He looks up at me with a sheepish expression on his face. "I… Umm…"

"Can you put weight on your feet you think?"

He feels around the side of the mostly destroyed chair, as if looking for something to hold onto.

"Here, take my hands," I tell him.

"There's no way. You won't be able to hold me."

Remembering how he reacted earlier when I was bossing him around, I straighten myself and repeat myself in a much firmer tone.

"Take. My. Hands. Now."

He stops hesitating and does as he's told.

"Try to scoot forward."

He shuffles left and right, wincing as he does so. His already bruised skin must burn, rubbing past that splintered wood. Still, I don't see any other way this will work.

"Now, lean forward and see how your feet take it."

"They're tingling real bad."

I let go of his hands and kneel down in front of him to massage his calves and feet. They're super puffy and swollen. I rub the bottom of his feet with my palm, trying to get his blood to circulate better. All the while, I look up at him to see how he's doing. His face is damp with sweat now. Despite having more room in his chair, he still struggles to take deep breaths. I wish I knew how to help him with that. Maybe once I get him out of this filth, he will feel better. Hopefully. But if he can't get up… shit. He simply has to. I certainly can't lift him. Worst case, he'll have to crawl out of here.

"Okay let's try again," I say, while getting up and taking his hands. "See if you can lean forward for me and get some of your weight onto your feet."

He scoots forward again, huffing and puffing as he does, then leans towards me while I pull at both of his hands. That seems to help some. For a moment it seems like he might lose his balance and fall forward into me but he catches himself. I pull his arms up and guide them around my shoulders, then I try to get my hands behind his back somehow. We both put our backs into it. The chair groans in protest, and more wood splinters away from where I'd cut the armrests off. The chair rocks forward along with him. I push against the backrest as hard as I can. That seems to work. There's a loud sound that reminds of fabric tearing as his backside releases off the chair and he's up. Sort of. He's bent forward at an awkward angle. And I'm sure he's in quite a lot of pain right now.

His breathing is shallow and quick and I think he might be crying again. He's sweating like a pig and his shoulders and back are trembling. I'm sure his legs and knees must be doing that too; I just can't see from where I am. This must be impossibly hard.

"You're doing it! Zach you're up!" I rub his shoulder encouragingly as he tries to straighten himself.

"I can't… I can't!" He's frozen in place, but his head is swaying just a little. I hold onto him as tightly as I can. He's obviously way too heavy for me, but I figure, this might help just a bit. His head rests against mine; his breaths tickle against the side of my neck.

"Baby, you can do it. This is all you now."

"I'm–I'm gonna fall…" He's panting so hard now he's almost hyperventilating.

"I've got you. Rest your head against me if you need to. Focus on how your feet feel, standing flat on the cold floor." I'm rambling. Not sure if any of what I'm saying makes any sense to him. He must be so dizzy, after all those days without food or water. Whenever I get dizzy, usually after a few too many drinks, it always helps me to focus on grounding my feet.

At the very least he's hugging me, and he's standing still, somewhat. His head rests heavy on my shoulder, though he's still trembling all over. As soon as he's somewhat stable, we need to move quickly. If we don't, he'll definitely fall over and we'll be so screwed.

"Zach, let's head towards the bedroom. One foot after the other, come on."

He tries to shuffle towards me, and straightens his back just a little. He's taller than me, which totally isn't helpful in this current situation. I can hear his joints crack as he tries to move. God, he must be so cramped. I wish I knew how to help right now, but this is something he has to do mostly on his own.

"You're doing great, come on!" I tell him. Finally, he's standing more upright. It's actually striking how big he is. I'm taken aback by how imposing he looks. But his face is still so vulnerable. He's the same old Zach, completely unaware of how impressed I am right now at what he's already achieved. But this is just the start.

He lets go of me, sort of, allowing me to get next to him. Only one of his arms remains anchored across my shoulder for support. And then he starts to walk. Tiny little steps at a time. Slowly but surely, we're getting away from that god-awful chair, or what's left of it, and approach the hallway leading to the rest of the flat. As soon as he reaches the nearest wall, he rests his other hand against it and pauses to catch his breath.

"We're gonna make it," I tell him.

"Thanks to you."

I shake my head. "Oh no, this is all you now."

He glances over at me. "Why are you doing this? I mean…"

I squeeze the hand which continues to linger on my shoulder. "Don't you worry about that. Let's get you into the other room, alright?"

He nods and starts walking ever so slowly again. The exertion is written all over his face. I just hope and pray that his body can take it.

"Tell me about yourself, Zach."

"There's nothing…" he says.

"What are your interests? What do you like?" A part of me is just trying to distract him with conversation. But a growing part of me truly wants to know. How did he end up like this? How did he live before? Where did that psycho, Jared come from? Do I need to worry about the guy actually turning up and hurting the both of us, especially now that I've switched his video feed off?

"Ah, I guess I'm a bit of a nerd. Star Wars. Fantasy novels..."

He's struggling to speak in full sentences while walking, but that's understandable. I wish I could do more to help, but I really can't. He's just so big; so heavy. He's going to have to get where we're going all on his own steam. All I can do is make sure nothing gets in the way, and to offer my body as support.

As we make our way through the hallway, I pause at the bathroom. There was a sturdy looking chair in the shower there. One of those white numbers you see disabled people use. And he is very ripe after sitting in his own filth for who knows how long... I push open the door, and he starts shuffling towards it, one laboured step at a time pretty much on autopilot. Or maybe he's looking forward to sitting down for a moment as well.

Every step is still so laboured; so slow, but he seems to speed up at the sight of the chair that's sitting in the center of the wet room. But I can't let him sit just yet. While we're here, we're going to make the most of it.

"Strip off."

"No way," Zach protests.

"Come on, let's get you cleaned up at least?"

He looks away from me, sweat-stained and exhausted, with a lost expression on his face. I don't know what's going through his mind, but it's not anything positive. Does he think I'll judge him after everything we've just achieved?

Just the pants. If he just gets rid of those, then the rest will be easy enough. I start pulling on them, ignoring the dirt that's obscuring their original colour. He sways a little, side to side, about to lose his balance, but then catches himself against the wall and helps me peel the waistband off his inflamed skin. All the dirt solidified over time, making the fabric rough and rigid and also stuck to him in places. It must hurt, but we have to get rid of it nonetheless.

He winces as we both pull it off him, a couple of inches first, then the rest of the way over his swollen thighs and buttocks. I try not to focus on the smell, or the sight of the soiled clothes or what lays beneath. While he's still up, in an awkwardly bent position, I take the shower head off the holder and turn on the water, waiting for just the right temperature.

Luckily the stream of water is strong, and it gets warm pretty quickly, allowing me to hose him off from behind.

"Here, wash yourself," I tell him, while handing him a half-empty bottle of shower gel off the shelf behind us.

He's keeping his eyes fixed on the ground while hurriedly squeezing the soap into his hand and rubbing it on himself. He won't be able to stay like this for long, his knees are starting to tremble even more now. But with another well-aimed jet of water on his backside, at least he's clean enough for the first time in God knows how long. I get rid of the evidence of his shame with the water, forcing all the muck into the drain on the floor.

"You can sit now," I tell him.

He lets out a loud groan as he lowers himself. His knees crack loudly in the process.

"Please..." he begs. "Please, you can go now. I've got this."

His eyes are flagging again, he's so exhausted. If I leave him now, he'll just be stuck sitting here for much too long, wet and catching a cold.

I shake my head. Instead, I grab his toothbrush and hand it to him after squeezing some paste onto it and wetting it in the stream of water from the shower. We're doing this; and we're doing it properly and quicker than he could do by himself.

He reluctantly starts to brush his teeth, while I carefully direct the water onto his head and letting it cascade down his body. He seems to like that, because he's leaning back a little now and closing his eyes. In any case, he's not freaking out anymore. His movements slow and within a minute or so, he's not brushing anymore. I suppose that's probably enough anyway. I take the brush and give him water to rinse.

He opens his eyes and studies me for a moment. "I guess I'm done."

I smile at him briefly. Nope. We're not done. This was just the bare fucking minimum.

But at least now that the worst is washed away, the bathroom smells pleasingly of soap, and it even looks somewhat clean now that the dust that had previously covered the floor has been rinsed into the drain. And that, along with the rather impressive looking overhead shower that's fitted right above us, is inspiring me to do things I would have never considered only moments earlier.

I step aside before switching the water from the hand shower to the overhead one, and then I start pulling at his wet t-shirt, peeling it off his belly and tugging at the back of it until he gets the message and leans forward a little, to get it off his back.

"We're done when I say we're done," I tell him in as calm a voice as I can manage. But actually, I'm getting more than a little excited by what lies ahead. I won't do anything inappropriate, of course, but...

It would be a lie to pretend like this large man, sitting here exposed in such a vulnerable position, isn't inspiring some deep dark thoughts in me. And he is rather handsome, now that he isn't so dirty anymore.

I'm going to wash him. Thoroughly. Lovingly. I'm going to wash every inch of him like a mother might wash a baby. Except, he's so much bigger than a baby, and some of the urges I feel are distinctly unmotherly.

The only thing that could be construed as motherly instinct of sorts is my determination to *love* him. To care for him. To give him all the things that he hasn't gotten from anyone, least of all that Jared motherfucker he keeps referring to. Now that we've left the horrors of what awaited me in the living room behind, I find that I'm not actually repulsed by him. Quite the opposite.

Now that I've got him in this rather intimate setting, completely exposed ever since his t-shirt has come off, he's rather enticing to me. His large body which had outgrown that chair we destroyed together. The vast canvas of his skin, which might have stretched over his bulk more tautly only days ago when he had his last meal prior to my arrival. The various folds and ripples, mounds and valleys which I intend to explore in minute detail, aided by a healthy dose of soap and water.

He's red in the face, his arms crossed in front of himself, as if he's desperately hanging onto some semblance of modesty. My sweet boy, we're well beyond that now.

But, not one to enjoy the discomfort of others, I start to undress as well. So we're even. Equal. Naked in front of each other, with nothing left to hide. Plus, I'm pretty sweaty myself now, so I could use a shower as well.

I feel his eyes linger on my most prominent features; my perky breasts with pale pink nipples already standing to attention, and my curvaceous ass, which I've always been rather proud of as well. It makes me heat up right into my core, to know that he's watching me just as I've been watching him.

All his talk of Jared this; Jared that; had made me wonder if he's into girls at all. It appears that these worries may have been unfounded. He's definitely interested, though he's pretending to look away now. From the corner of his eye, he's still checking me out in secret.

And I love it. God, I love it. I want him to see me. To admire me. And I want to admire him right back.

Now the warm water is steaming up the bathroom, giving it a mysterious sort of atmosphere. Sensual. Sexy, even. I turn the water down for a moment, to give me more time to live out my plans for him.

He tries to clear his throat, but doesn't say anything. Emboldened by his silence, I squeeze some shower gel into my palm and start rubbing it onto his shoulders, which tense up. He's got some serious issues with people touching him. I want to ask why, but that might only make him more self conscious. Instead, I start massaging him. His neck, with the deep fold at the back, where his back flesh pushes upwards against the base of his scalp... Those muscles connecting his shoulders to his neck, which are rock hard and probably quite painful after the exertion I've put him through just to get here.

In even, circular motions, I rub his shoulder blades and that fleshy bit on either side of his spine; at least the parts of him that are sticking up over the backrest of the chair. I take his arm, and apply more soap to it, as well as his armpit and lather up the little patch of hair that awaits underneath. Then, I repeat the motion on the other side.

The shower gel smells intoxicating; like a magical flower meadow, where anything is possible. And it is, because he's letting me do whatever I want now without argument.

I squeeze some on myself and make it foam up, enjoying the sensation of the lather slipping down my tits and onto my stomach and down my thighs.

Moving in front of him again, I rub some soap into his chest, where tufts of brown hair make it foam up even more when I massage him. I make sure to be thorough, lifting up his rather substantial tits and wash carefully and gently underneath each one. Also, between all the folds on his sides. One, two, three, with a fourth, much bigger one around the crotch area, but I leave that one for later.

As I carry on, I can see him relax underneath my touch. I can feel it, too. His shoulders, which were so very tight before, are slumping downwards now when I rub them again. His breaths are deepening and the creases on his forehead are smoothing over. Even the tightness in his lips is reducing until they're slightly parted and looking oh so inviting despite how dry and damaged they looked earlier.

I grab the shampoo off the shelf and apply a healthy amount of it to his head, working my fingertips into his scalp as I spread it around. I massage him around the temples, behind the ears, at the base of his skull and on the top of his crown. Working away at him, until he is so relaxed, his head is wobbling around a little. I position myself behind him, coaxing him to tilt his head back against my belly, making sure none of the shampoo ends up in his eyes.

Then I lean down and kiss him on the forehead, which prompts him to open them and look up at me, still in silence, right past the two mounds of my breasts and into my eyes.

"You're going to be okay," I tell him, while hugging my arm around the front of his chest and pressing my naked, slippery body up against his back. "Everything's going to be okay, sweetheart."

A soft gasp escapes his lips when I wash the side of his neck, the top of his chest, even though I'd done that bit already. It's so nice to feel him slip and slide against me. It's such a tactile experience...

"You don't have to do this," he whispers. His voice is cracking as he speaks, but at least he's breathing better now and not coughing nearly so much. The steam must be helping him in more ways than I'd hoped.

"Zach, don't worry about a thing. I'm here now. I'll take care of you."

I release him just enough to be able to move towards his front again, rubbing, massaging, soaping him up all over as I go. It feels so good, how his soft pillowy flesh gives way underneath my touch. I never thought I'd like this as much as I do. It's by far the most erotic experience of my life.

His eyes are shut again, and his breaths more intense and deeper. He's leaning back in the chair now, giving me better access to his belly and all the wondrous folds and ripples of flesh on his sides.

There, where the waistband of his pants used to be, the skin is bright red and angry looking. I take special care to wash it ever so gently, and not damage him further. Still, it probably burns, because he inhales sharply whenever I move my hand past it, causing his whole body to jiggle with every breath.

I've never seen anything like it. He's like a great big pile of jelly. I'm getting awfully close to wondering what other pleasures his body could give me. Maybe, with him lying on his back and me on top...

No, that would be wrong. I'm here to help him, not to take advantage of him! All he seems to know are people who wanted to do him harm. I don't wish for that. I just want to show him love and affection.

I kneel down in front of him, soaping up his feet, which are tense and stiff underneath my touch. His calves are tense too. Or they're probably just cramped, after having to carry his weight for the first time in ages. I pick up his foot, prompting him to stretch his leg out in front of him. He struggles to do so. All the simple movements I take for granted are a chore for him.

My heart weeps for everything he's had to endure. I so wish I could take his pain away. I wish...

And so I pour all those wishes into giving him a thorough foot and calf massage. I slide my fingers in between his toes, spreading them a little, and rub his tired flesh, trying to take all his aches and pains away.

When I pick up his other foot to repeat the process all over again, he tries to scoot forward a little on the chair, stretching his leg out again. And then... Almost with a mind of its own, his hand, which had so far been hanging limply on the side of his body, starts to travel up his thigh and into...

He's sighing rather than breathing now. Deeply in and out. His big belly shifting up and down with every breath. And from my vantage point in front of him, down on my knees, when he spreads his legs apart and slips his hand into the soapy depths of his crotch, I'm rewarded with a glimpse of thick, hard cock.

He moans softly while he fondles it, almost as if he doesn't realise what he's doing.

Maybe he doesn't. Maybe he's so exhausted now that he's slipped into a beautiful dream. One which I would love to live out with him. But first... I don't think he did a very good job washing himself down there. He was too ashamed, and in too much of a rush.

I put some more soap on my hand and start by rubbing it into the big fold that runs right underneath his belly. Then, as I massage the foam into him, deeper and deeper I go, until our hands touch, and he freezes.

But when slip in underneath his fingers, soaping up his erection and his balls, as well as all the wonderfully soft flesh surrounding it all, he spreads his thighs apart wider, and even tilts his hips upward to give me more room.

Throughout these explorations, with me kneeling on the soapy tile floor in between his thick tree-trunk-like legs, I feel myself getting more and more aroused. I didn't think it possible, but I'm creaming all over myself while stimulating him.

I've never had this reaction before while jerking off a man. And I'm not even going at it very hard just yet. I'm still just feeling it. Stroking it. Loving it, and him along with it.

His cock isn't very big, at least not compared to the rest of him. And it's mostly hidden there in the dark, invisible and unloved. At least that's what I'm imagining as it's growing further underneath my touch.

Unloved and neglected like he is. There will be no more of that, as long as I'm here. I'll make sure he is taken care of in every way possible.

No longer content on my knees, I get up and turn the water up too, then, with one hand still grasping at his cock, and the other rubbing and washing the soap off of his chest, I lower myself down onto one of his substantial thighs, straddling him as though I'm sitting on horseback. And then I tighten my grip around his fat little dick, prompting him to open his eyes and stare at me. Into me.

"Lindsey, no." His eyebrows are raised in shock, but every time I pump his cock with my hand, his expression falters and calms ever so slightly.

"Relax. Let me love you," I tell him.

"You can't."

Though he's protesting, he hasn't made an effort to move me off him. Quite the opposite. His other hand, which had been idle previously, ends up on my lower back, just at the start of the curvature of my ass. It's delicious, making me shift forward on his thigh, rubbing my cunt into him.

"Zach, my love, I just want to make you feel good."

His fingers dig into my ass cheek, and he lets out a loud, desperate groan. Then, his other hand makes its way back to his cock, surrounding my hand, and forcing me into a faster rhythm.

"Baby, not yet," I whisper in his ear.

"I'm sorry," he whimpers. "This is so bad, but I can't help it."

He's really gagging for it now. Not surprising. He must have been so lonely, waiting on someone who never came.

"You're not bad," I tell him, while leaning in to kiss his neck.

He cries out and wraps his arm around my back,

pressing our wet naked bodies against each other, with both our hands trapped in between, in the hot depths of his crotch. And then he starts pumping himself harder with my hand. It's actually exhilarating, how much strength he can muster for this. And what speed.

I couldn't escape his grip if I wanted to; despite reaching the limits of his strength on the way here, he is still way stronger than I am.

"Zach, you're gorgeous. You're perfect just as you are." I tell him, while gripping him more firmly myself now. No longer am I just a passive participant in his feverish attempts to get himself off, but now, I'm the instigator again.

"I love your thick hard cock, Zach. I love how horny you are right now."

"Ohhh."

When he moans, loudly and desperately; the sound amplified by the echo of the tiled bathroom, I feel myself getting more horny as well. I'm actually getting close, something that's never happened to me before without so much as a finger or a tongue at my clit.

What is there, though, is a great big fat thigh, squishy and glorious, pressing against my entire private area. Or rather, my body weight is pressing it into him, which feels amazing.

I rock my hips just so, getting the angle just right, and cry out his name.

"Zach! You're going to make me cum!"

He opens his eyes again, wide in surprise, when I grab his fat face and press my lips into his.

The resulting sensations are too much for me to bear. Our kiss undoes me. I tense up, squeezing down hard on his cock which has been in my hand all this time. I wrap my legs around his thigh as well, grinding and rubbing against him...

His arm around my back drags me closer against him. Our mouths, seemingly starved for each other, remain fused while our tongues try desperately to show the other just how much we needed this.

Not just him, but me also.

We continue to kiss, sloppy messy wet kisses, almost like we're trying to eat each other out, but at the wrong end.

It's beautiful. It's glorious. I feel triumphant.

My body is buzzing with sensations I've never thought possible. And it's all due to him.

And he's right there with me. His big fat body shuddering and trembling against me. Soft jiggly flesh, exaggerating every breath and moan and gasp of his. And his thick cock in my hand, quivering as it spurts hot semen into my fingers.

And then... Silence. All is still, save for the sound of the water bearing down on us from the shower, while we remain seated, arms and legs entwined, just breathing into each other's faces, waiting for our hearts to quieten.

I let go of him, and gently slip my hand out from in between us, letting the warm water wash away his cum, watching as it floats across the floor and into the drain.

He retreats from our embrace, averting his gaze from me while washing his own right hand. That is, until I embrace him, hugging him tightly against me again, and resting my head against his.

"Zach," I say, loving how the inside of my chest tickles when I say his name. "Zach, baby, I've never felt like this before. I've never done anything like this before."

He grunts something unintelligible. Have I made a terrible mistake? Have I taken advantage of him too, just like everyone else?

I pull away and see that he's crying again. It's quite a sight, now that I think about it. Such a big man, crying so openly in front of me pretty much ever since I got to his place. I suppose he's too exhausted to be ashamed of it. Having had too much to be ashamed of already all in one day.

"I'm sorry, I didn't mean to upset you," I whisper, while loosening my arms around his neck. "I just wanted to make you feel good."

He looks at me, briefly, then looks away again. "You didn't."

Yeah, this was a terrible misjudgement on my part. My heart sinks when I let go of him, and try to scoot back to get up off his thigh.

"You didn't upset me," he says, resting his hand tentatively on top of mine and stopping my retreat in its tracks. "I just don't get it. Why are you doing all this?"

"I just... When I look at you, there's something in your eyes. Something that tells me to take things too far, maybe."

He shakes his head. "I've never done this either. I've

never had anyone to--"

"You're not gay, are you?" I ask, almost afraid to hear the answer. Despite all the physical feedback he's been giving me. Despite the way he continues to steal glances down at my tits.

"No!"

"I just thought, because of Jared... It seems like a weird arrangement otherwise."

He sighs and shakes his head. "I'd posted a video, asking for help. I've always struggled with my weight and everything else. My whole life."

"Okay."

"I knew it wouldn't lead anywhere good. I knew that left to my own devices-- I was afraid to die alone in this flat, you know? I don't have any family. No friends... Who would even notice once I was gone?"

"Oh sweetheart," I hug him tightly, without even thinking about whether I'm making things worse or not. But he hugs me back, moaning softly again as my hands caress his upper back. God he's so big. I'd need at least two more pairs of hands just to do him justice.

Maybe he doesn't hate being touched after all. He's just so starved for affection, it was too intense for him without realizing what pleasures it could lead to.

"He told me he was a personal trainer. He'd help me lose weight; I was to be his biggest achievement. He set some challenges for me, to build up my self control... But I failed, I..." Zach stammers.

"Challenges?"

"He made me download some software to get

control over the webcam, so he could monitor my progress... And every day, he would order the most tempting food and I had to learn to resist it. But I never could. I can't control myself around food, which is why I'm in this mess in the first place."

"Zach, sweetheart!" I plant kisses on his forehead, his cheeks, his lips. He's such a beautiful soul. He trusted this guy and all he got in return was sick games and trickery. I can't imagine the kind of person who would stoop so low.

"He convinced me to sit in that chair, though I hadn't used it in ages, ever since I outgrew it. And after failing so many times to resist the food he got me... He said I had to, that it would help me get in shape to practice sitting in it. Well, then you can imagine what happened."

"It's okay now. It's all going to be okay," I tell him, while kissing the side of his neck some more. He leans into my kisses, trapping my face between his head and his shoulder ever so gently, which makes me smile.

"Since I was stuck at that point, he told me it was time for the next phase. He would teach me how to fast, so that I could lose the weight that way." He's leaving so much unspoken. Four days between the pizza order and the delivery I brought. Four entire days of starvation. How many days' gap was there between the pizza and his last meal before that? I can't bear to think about it.

"Baby, I'm so sorry. He should never have done these things to you." I caress him, hold him, cradle his head in my arms. All the while, he hugs me back, clinging to me like I'm the only thing that matters anymore. It's intoxicating to be this close to him. To feel him this intensely.

"He said he was going to help me. But I guess I brought it all on myself. I'm such a fucking idiot."

"It's not your fault." I pull away again, and he releases me instantly. It almost hurts where his hands used to be only a second ago. I realize I'm crying as well now. "Look at me, Zach."

He glances up at me, briefly.

"Baby, none of this is your fault. It's his."

"He must be so angry that the feed is off." Zach sniffles softly, then looks away from me again.

"He can fuck right off. I'm in a good mood to call the cops on him for what he's done."

"But... How will I-- What will I do?"

"Here's what we'll do, sweetheart. We're going to get you dried off and dressed, and get you into bed. And you don't have to worry about anything. I'll take care of it."

He nods quietly.

"Won't it feel good to be lying in your own bed again?" I ask him.

He sighs a couple of times, loudly, his shoulders slumping down low as he does so. Poor guy, he looks so shattered. But soon, he won't have to be. Soon, he'll be able to rest and recover.

I lean over to switch off the water. The silence is deafening. Except for his continued breaths, which are quite a bit louder than any normal person I've ever heard. I guess that's just what he sounds like normally, because now that he isn't coughing anymore, I can't hear any wheezes or rattles anymore either.

The hot water has done him good. Both of us, actually. The soreness in my hands and arms from sawing through that chair has started to fade as well.

Upon getting off his thigh, I grab a towel from the rack and drape it across his shoulders, then I grab another to wrap around myself.

"Can you wait here for a minute? Then we'll go."

He stares at me, his expression tense and lips pressed tightly against themselves.

"I'm not leaving you," I reassure him, and his face calms just a little. "I'll be *right* back."

He must be so terrified of being let down again. It sounds like he'd latched onto that asshole with all his hope, only to be taken advantage of in the most horrible way. I won't do that to him. Ever. No, I'm going to make sure he can rest, and I'm going to get his place sorted out a bit. And then... Well, I guess we'll figure it out together. All I know is that I'm not leaving him.

With the towel wound around me tightly so I don't drip everywhere, I rush down the hallway and into the bedroom. The sheets are a bit dusty, but it's not so bad. I clear the bed, fluff up the pillows, shake off the duvet and clear the clutter off the floor. Not bad for a couple of minutes worth of effort. And then I check his closet for a fresh change of clothes.

T-shirt and shorts seem fine.

There's a hairbrush on a chest of drawers by the wall,

I carry that with me too.

Armed with these necessities, I enter the bathroom again, where Zach is waiting, suddenly looking very fragile and sad again. I take the towel off his shoulders and start by drying his hair and brushing it. He already looks so much better; with his damp locks framing his face.

Then I dab the water off his shoulders, his chest, his back and arms and sides. Slowly and carefully, I dry off his torso; or at least as much of it as I can reach with the chair in the way. And then, I place the towel over his legs, dabbing at his thighs, his calves...

My own towel untucks and opens up, allowing him a fresh look at my damp tits while my long dark hair sticks to my face and shoulders.

He shifts in his seat, spreading his thighs again like he did when we were showering. Is he getting hard again, I wonder? I could certainly go again...

But instead of trying my luck just yet, I just keep drying him off until he's all done. And then I hand him his t-shirt. His hand trembles as he tries to take it from me, but I snatch it away at the last second.

"You know, I think I prefer you like this. I should probably wear it instead," I tell him, with a naughty smile on my lips.

He smiles back at me when I put it on, staining the fresh cotton with the droplets that were still clinging to my skin. I'd put all my efforts into drying him off, forgetting myself in the process.

"How's it look?" I ask him, gathering the excess

fabric around my slender waist, and twirling around in front of him. It's so very big, even in the neck, that it almost looks like a flowy dress, swooping neckline and all.

What I like best about it is that it's his. So this is what his scent should have been... Delicious. Comforting.

"Perfect. You're beautiful," he tells me.

I lean over and kiss him on the lips. "So are you." Normally, this is the sort of thing I'd say automatically. Something you say because you don't want to make the other person feel less than. But in this case, I'm not filled with the kind of hidden guilt that accompanies such a statement. I'm not lying. I'm not pretending.

I mean it. To me, he's perfect just as he is.

He shakes his head, probably because he's unwilling to hear me. I decide not to argue with him and gesture at him to get up.

It's a struggle, but nothing like what we had to go through in the living room. He leans forward and with an almighty groan, he shifts his weight onto his feet while I help by pulling at his arms. Now, with better access to his rear, I dry off the rest of him. The ripples and folds on his back; his rather magnificently huge jiggly ass... Then, I invite him to step forward onto a dry bit of floor, and make him get into his shorts.

His body is unlike anything I've ever seen up close. Where regular guys are flat and boring, he has all this extra flesh. All these little crevices and folds. I never realized how much I'd appreciate a physique like his.

Neither does he, probably. I was in a good mood to keep him entirely nude, but I fear that would be too mean. I help him pull the shorts over his calves and up his thighs. They're so big, I'm sure both my whole body could fit into one of their legs. That thought excites me even further. Would I even be able to spread wide enough to get him in between my thighs, should we, you know, do the deed?

Jesus, what's happened to me all of a sudden? My mind has ended up in the gutter ever since... Since getting him naked, I suppose. I don't even know where else these dirty ideas could be coming from!

"Okay, into the bedroom we go," I encourage him.

He huffs and puffs with every step. I kind of like the sound now. It reminds me of when he was almost going to cum. He sounds like he's always at his limit; like everything about him is turned to eleven. And my arousal is up there right along with him.

It takes us a full five minutes, or thereabouts, just to make the journey down the hallway and into his bedroom. Once there, I direct him towards the bed, steady his arm as he positions himself and sits down, and help him put his legs up when he lies down on his side.

I'm putting the duvet over him when he suddenly grabs my wrist.

"I'm sorry for being such a bother," he tells me.

I smile down at him and caress his damp hair with my other hand. "Don't even worry about it."

He closes his eyes, but his grip on my arm doesn't

loosen.

"Baby, I'm going to need you to let go."

"No, please."

"I'm not leaving you. I would never," I tell him. "In fact, I think I would rather like to join you under the covers."

His eyes open again, and he tries to scoot back on the bed, giving me room. It's rather hopeless, though and he ends up trapped on his back.

"It's okay, I'll get in from the other side."

He watches me as I peel the duvet back on the empty side of the bed, and get in. He's so warm and so soft. And his bare skin is so tempting. He lets out a loud groan when he struggles to turn over on his other side, facing me. I manage to slip my arm underneath his neck, so his head rests on my shoulder and his arms engulf me. He's so damn big, he surrounds me, pretty much. Warm, slightly damp, gorgeously soft skin. His tits are huge too, he actually has quite a substantial amount of cleavage at this angle. And his belly pushes into my side heavily with every breath.

I caress his face. I don't think I'll ever tire of looking into these deep blue eyes. So innocent, how he keeps staring at me, full of wonder.

"I'd never kissed anyone before..." he whispers. "Never held anyone like this..."

"I couldn't tell. You're a natural," I say, while putting my other arm around his waist; well, around the fold in his side where his waist would have been. My hand doesn't get very far around him. Most of him is totally out of my reach. How I wish I could make him feel as good; as loved as he makes me feel when he hugs me. It's such an overwhelming experience how he dwarfs me and makes me feel safe.

But I can caress his hair, and hold him around his neck. He kisses the side of my face, just whatever part is right in front of him. His hand rests on my stomach. I take it, and nudge it up a little. Just enough. Just until it reaches my chest.

He moans when he grabs my tit, and not to be outdone, I grab his. They're so big; so heavy. Much bigger than mine. I think I love that too. Great big tits, and a great big belly. I fondle his body, squeezing and massaging various parts of him; I'm not even sure what exactly I'm playing with at any moment, only that it's wonderful.

He's got his eyes shut again, and tugs the shirt up and over my naked body until his hand has a free rein over my bare chest. And then, almost without warning, his face travels downward, inching closer to my nipple. Until with what must be the last ounce of strength he has left, he raises himself up and guides my boob into his mouth.

He licks and suckles on me, setting my insides on fire all over again. It's so intense and yet so very gentle; so unlike anything I've ever experienced. And the sensation is only heightened by the soft scratch of his beard against my chest.

Is he reliving something long since forgotten? Trying to get a comfort only reserved for the very young? Or maybe it's worse than that. Maybe this is something that's always been withheld from him?

I catch myself moaning now, along with him, while he continues to suck on me, massaging me with his tongue, and fondling me with his hand. All the while, I pick up one of his tits in my hand, marvelling again at how heavy it is. How full. I roll his nipple between my thumb and index finger, causing him to moan even louder and jerk his hips in my direction until he settles into a smooth motion of rocking back and forth into me.

Is he getting himself off like this? I reach downward and try to find out. But there's so much flesh in the way, I'm finding it hard to figure out where his cock is hidden exactly. I do know he's enjoying himself. The sounds he's making are clear as day.

I've never been with anyone this vocal. He couldn't keep quiet even if he tried. As if he's feeling it all so much more intensely than other people. Maybe because it's the first time. Because surely that's what that meant. I was his first kiss. And now we're in bed, cuddling and rubbing up against each other.

His first.

I wish he was mine, because everyone who came before is a pale comparison to the glory before me right now.

He's a marvel. A treasure. He's paradise personified.

And I want nothing more than to--

His tongue flicks against my nipple just right. Again and again and again, while he carries on suckling on me.

And his other hand tries to replicate the motion on my other nipple. It drives me wild. I wedge my hand in under his big belly, feeling my way towards his crotch. There it is. Surrounded by soft flesh, a hard rod of pleasure, waiting to be unleashed.

I grab his balls, firmly but not harshly, like I know a lot of guys enjoy, and then I massage his foreskin over the head of his cock. He speeds up, rubbing himself into his own skin folds, against my hand and into my hip.

"Oh god, you're killing me!" I whine. He keeps licking me; keeps sucking on me. It's too much. Too intense. And then, he suddenly lets go of my tit, and reaches downward. His hand rests heavily on my mound, and his index finger starts feeling around right in between the fold.

"Holy shit, right there!" I scream. He curls his finger right up to my clit. "Wiggle it!" I instruct. He does so, and within seconds of his continued teasing, I come apart, screaming his name.

Meanwhile he's rutting into me still, as fast and as hard as he can in his current state. I put my hand on his shoulder and try to push him back. But obviously I can't even hope to shift his bulk.

"Get on you back," I tell him, but he doesn't react to that either.

"On your back!" I order him, still out of breath and out of sorts, but in as a firm a tone as I can manage. His eyes snap open and he retreats.

"I'm sorry. I'm sorry. I'm sorry."

I shake my head and smile lazily. Jesus, that orgasm

nearly levelled me. "Don't be sorry. Be on your back."

He turns, and I climb on top. Astride his thighs, I try to find the gap where I know his crotch to be, spreading his flesh apart carefully so I don't hurt his already inflamed skin, and wedging my thighs in there deeply. My wet cunt ends up in exactly the right spot, with his fat cock tickling the entrance. And then I push down.

His eyes roll into the back of his head and he makes the most beautiful, guttural sounds.

"Ohhh!"

"Ahhh!"

With every thrust of mine, he continues to sing. His hand reaches up, back up to the boob he'd been sucking on earlier. Somehow, despite having no experience at all, he knows how to touch me just gently enough to stimulate me without hurting me. His hands are magic.

I could do this forever, except I know he's in dire need of relief. And I couldn't last long before my next one either. So, I don't even try to drag it out much. I buck my hips with every push, revelling in how the fluffy fat around his dick presses up against my clit when he's deep inside of me.

Anchoring myself with both hands on the roundest part of his belly, I carry on riding him. In and out. Up and down. Until his eyes briefly open again, our gaze meets, and I can't help but smile while crying out his name.

"Zach! You're gonna make me cum!"

His body straightens like a plank, and his hips shudder up into me. All of his flesh, jiggling and moving just stimulates me further. I tighten my pelvic muscles as hard as I can, which sends me flying over the edge of bliss. Right to where he's already waiting for me.

He cries and laughs and groans and gasps for air. His body shudders and twitches, and his cock seems to gush a big fucking load right into my core. And it doesn't stop either. Not like regular guys. He's cumming for what feels like forever. Twitching and spurting, trembling and spraying some more. I imagine it looking like a fire hose, dousing me, quenching my thirst, satisfying my hunger all at once.

Then, I lower myself onto him, into his already open arms, and I'm home.

"Shit, that was amazing," I whimper, still shivering, because that's pretty much taken everything out of me.

I can't imagine how he feels, after cumming into me so hard, I could sense every drop of it. His embrace tightens around me, and there's nowhere I'd rather be.

No matter how today started, or maybe more so because it was so grim. This was a righteous end to it. Or rather, is it a beginning? Because I'm still straddling him; his cock is still inside of me and still somewhat firm; and I have no intention of changing that any time soon.

Content, sweaty and sated, I close my eyes and nestle into his gorgeously fleshy man cleavage, while listening to the feverish beat of his heart, and his quick and rather loud panting breaths.

And I thank my lucky stars that I was the one who took the order this morning. That I was the one who found him. Because I'm going to do everything I can to show him that life can be different. That people can be good. And that he is loved exactly the way he is.

Everything he's been through; all the pain other people have caused him. It's all in the past and I'll make sure it stays there.

From now on, it's just him and me. Nothing else matters. I'm going to get his place sorted out; and watch over him while he sleeps. I'll get some groceries ordered in to feed him properly. No more takeout and junk food and all the other shit he's been living off of. No more mind games and trickery, courtesy Jared the psycho.

When he wakes up, I'll be there to love him in every possible way. I'll hug him and kiss him and nurse him back to health. I wish to be the one he confides in; to express all his doubts and fears and hopes and dreams. I'll do what I can to make the latter come true. This is my purpose. This is the reason I was the one to deliver his order and not one of the other girls.

"I must be dreaming," Zach mumbles, while tightening his arm around me.

"If you are, then so am I."

He jerks awake, prompting me to raise myself up so I can look at him. There he is, already staring up at me with wide eyes. "Are you even real or have I imagined you?"

"Oh, Zach." I plant a sweet kiss on his lips, then another. He lets out a soft moan against my mouth. "Don't worry about a thing now. I've got you."

"I don't deserve you," he whimpers. "I'm sorry."

"No, baby. You're so very special."

"I keep waiting to wake up back in that chair, alone."

"Zach, sweetheart. When you wake up, it'll be right here, with my arms still around you. I promise."

His breaths, although calmer than before, are still laboured. He probably shouldn't fall asleep on his back like this. I raise myself up. His grasp on me falters as he watches me with tear-filled eyes. But rather than get up and leave like he's probably expecting me to, I tug on his arm to make him turn over again. Just like how we were earlier when we first got into bed. With my arm around his neck, and his head resting on my shoulder.

I caress his damp hair, running my fingers through it, grazing my fingernails softly past his scalp. As his breathing slows, and his hand finds its way around me, twitching ever so slightly whenever he exhales, I carry on whispering sweet nothings at him.

"Zach, you're a treasure. I'm so glad I found you."

He moans softly, while readjusting himself and cuddling against me.

"Now that I've got you, I'm never ever going to leave."

"I think I love you," he mumbles, under his breath.

Overcome with emotions, I hug him against me tighter, but never stop caressing his hair. I was right all along. Despite the larger than life exterior, and the very adult urges and desires we've already lived out together, deep down he still is that scared little boy I saw in his eyes earlier. And I'll do everything in my power to take care of him.

First, we'll rest, then I'm going to I'm going to love him forever.

ABOUT THE AUTHOR

Dear Reader,

If you came across me in real life, you'd never guess the kind of filth I like to read and write. Cleverly disguised as a boring office worker, the drudgery of my 9-to-5 only becomes bearable because of my vivid and explicit imagination. I like fat guys and I cannot lie. In my world, bigger (fatter) is always better. It's been that way for as long as I can remember.

Thanks for reading this story, one of hopefully many of my published sexual fantasies. My stories revolve around one common theme: really big men and the women who can't help but lust for them.

Although I like porn just fine, it's nearly impossible to find it in the flavour that I desire. The written word allows me to explore a world of lush excess that mainstream adult entertainment just cannot provide. When I started writing, I soon discovered the beauty of having a catalog of erotica out there to satisfy my own lustful needs. This is a passion project more than a money-grab.

So, first and foremost, my writing is for me. But perhaps there are other women (or even men) out there who share my tastes; my fetishes and fantasies? My fascination with the larger male form, and sexualisation of food (especially overeating). If that sounds like something you'll wank off to, you've come to the right place.

xxx Hedonist

To find out more, check:

❖   eXplicitTales.com